I0676685

A Nation Divided

KENNY GORDON

Copyright © 2012 Kenny Gordon

All rights reserved.

ISBN: 978-0-9848307-0-1

AUTHOR'S NOTE

This novel is a work of fiction. Any reference to actual events, real people, living or dead, or to real locations is intended only to give the novel a sense of reality and authenticity. All of the names, characters, places and incidents are either the product of the author's imagination or are used fictitiously and their resemblance, if any, to real-life encounters, is entirely coincidental.

CONTENTS

ACKNOWLEDGMENTS

I am totally grateful to everybody who read the summary of my story and gave me the confidence and love to write this story. A special thanks goes to my very good friend Kate Wilson who at the beginning encouraged me to write this novel; I'm glad she is my friend. To Oprah Winfrey for being an inspiration through her talk show, I thank you. Thank you to my co-workers at Gregory Lincoln Educational Center who read the summary of my novel and gave me a positive push and to one student by the name of Saul, who one day asked me about my novel, for he wanted to buy a copy. He gave me that added push to complete this novel. A special thanks goes out to my friend Kenneth Linton who believed in my writing and saw its worth, so much so that he sent it to his friend Spike Lee. To my parents, Lawrence and Ethel Gordon, who gave me the guidance I needed to become the person that I am, especially my father who believed in me at the beginning and never doubted me and my abilities. Last but surely not least I thank my God in heaven, for without Him I would not have been able to write this novel.

Since the 1800's, the black man has struggled in the United States. From the 1900's to the 1950's, everything was separate but not equal. The black man had to use different restrooms (which were in poor condition), he had to drink out of a different water fountain (water that came from the sewer) and attend separate schools which barely had enough books for each student. In the 1960's, the black man started to gain ground in respect and equal treatment under the leadership of Dr. Martin Luther King, Jr. In th9e 1980's, the black man started to lose ground under the Reagan administration. More than half of the inmates in prisons were black. More blacks than ever were living at the poverty line. Black-on-black crime increased at an all-time high. Drugs manifested themselves in the black neighborhoods at an alarming rate. In the 1990's, blacks became a target for police officers throughout the United States. Because of the rash of violence against blacks by police officers (mainly white) and no justice served for these offenses, riots broke out throughout the country. Race riots became commonplace until a war ensued.

CHAPTER 1

The year 2055, the date, Friday October 1. John Savage, a black businessman, was in his home having breakfast. John is smart and very handsome, young, six-foot and one-inch tall, somewhat medium-built (about 198 pounds) man in his mid-twenties. He has a light skin complexion and his hair is black and cut in a business style and he is a very business-like dresser, wearing a suit and tie. The breakfast menu consisted of coffee, toast, bacon, eggs, and juice, a typical breakfast. John is also a single man, a kind of playboy, who has women coming in and out of his apartment. The phone rang. John answered the phone.

"Hello," he said.

"Hi there," this sexy voice said.

"Hi," John also replied.

"How did you enjoy the ride?" said the sexy voice.

"It was pure heaven," John said. "Why did you leave so early this morning? I wanted you to have breakfast with me."

"I had to leave. I have an image to keep up," the voice said.

"I will let you off this time, but you will have to have breakfast with me one of these times, image or no," John said.

"Well, we'll see. Will I see you tonight?" asked the sexy voice.

"Sure, if you'd like," John replied.

"Same time?" the voice asked.

"Sure, same time," John answered. They both said their good-byes and hung up. Two minutes later the phone rang again. John answered, "Hello."

"What's up man?" It's Spencer Lewis, John's partner in business and best friend. They have been friends since high school. Spencer is not quite the ladies' man like John, but he could get a date every once in a while. Spencer is a smart, average-looking young man, about five-feet, eleven inches tall with a medium built body (weighing about 170 pounds). He's also in his mid-twenties. He dresses in business wear as well. He has a medium-skin complexion and his hair is black and cut in the style of a very neat and very low Afro.

"How was last night with Mayor Kelly?" referring to the sexy voice that called John earlier.

"Fine, just fine," John replied in a satisfied voice. "We are going to see each other again tonight."

"Sounds like love to me," Spencer said with a hint of laughter.

"No," John said with a hint of laughter. "We just enjoy each other's company."

"Sure," Spencer replied. "Well, John, I was calling to tell you I'm going to be a little late this morning."

"Why?" John asked.

"I have a little errand to run before coming in," Spencer said.

"Sure!" John replied, "See you when I see you."

"Right," Spencer said.

They both hung up. John finished his breakfast and left his apartment for work in a 2053 customized Porsche. John and Spencer are realtors and ex-army men. John made it to work where his secretary, Lunette, a tall, slim woman with a model-like body, met him. She is five-feet, seven inches tall and has long black wavy hair. She has a light skin complexion and hazel eyes. She and John had an affair once, but could not see eye to eye on things. But there is still a little love between them. She really runs the office.

"Here are your messages, John," she said, looking at him as if she could undress at that moment and make passionate love to him.

"Thanks," John said, not noticing how she was looking at him. He entered his office, made a phone call, and started his daily work routines. One hour later Spencer entered John's office.

"Hey guy," Spencer said.

"Where did you go this morning?" John asked with a hint of anger in his voice.

"Relax, man," Spencer replied. "I had to take care of a little business. I'm here now."

"Look, Bro, you are going to have to carry your end of the business responsibility or this partnership will dissolve."

"Okay, okay, keep your shirt on. I understand" Spencer said. "Let's go to work."

CHAPTER 2

The rest of the day went on as usual, with John and Spencer seeing clients and making deals. At the end of the workday, about five o'clock, John received a phone call from Mayor Kelly. They had agreed to meet at his place again later that night about eight o'clock. John promised to cook dinner for her and afterward it would be another night of great lovemaking. On his way out to leave for home to prepare the lovely meal for Mayor Kelly, John stopped in Spencer's office to wish him a nice evening.

"Spencer, I'm going home now. I have another date with Mayor Kelly," he said as he smiled.

"Don't you ever rest, John?" Spencer asked.

"I'll rest when I get old and gray, but right now I'm going to sow my wild oats while I can," he replied in a grim tone. John turned to walk out of Spencer's office, and then he remembered something he wanted to ask Spencer. John turned his attention back to Spencer.

"Spencer, how would you like to go flying with me this weekend?" John asked.

"Fly?" Spencer said in a somewhat nervous voice.

"Yes," John said, "fly. I thought we might fly over the neutral zone and back. You know, live dangerously for once."

"I don't know..," Spencer said with a sense of caution.

"Sure you do," John interrupted. Then he looked at his watch. "Oh, got to run. I will be at your apartment at about eight o'clock tomorrow morning, so be ready," John said as he was left the office. John walked out of Spencer's office and into the small lobby to Lunette's desk. Spencer walked to his office door. Lunette entered John's path of motion to also say good night in her own way. She reached out to hug John but he stopped her.

"No, Lunette," he said. "Let's not start something we know will not work." On that note John left the office leaving Lunette with a sad look on her face. Spencer was watching the whole act.

"Why don't you give me a chance at your love, Lunette?" Spencer asked smiling. She looked at him and smiled back, then went back to her desk.

CHAPTER 3

John arrived home an hour after he left the office for he had to make a few stops to get the items he needed to make the dinner he promised the mayor. He usually got home in thirty minutes. He prepared a lovely Italian meal for her. The meal consisted of spaghetti with meat source, garlic bread, a salad with Italian dressing and a bottle of expensive white wine. John, in his younger days, learned how to prepare all kinds of dishes as a teenager when he worked as a cook's assistant. As he was putting the final touches on everything, the doorbell rang. John went to the door and opened it. Who else but Mayor Kelly was standing there in the doorway smiling?

She was a very attractive, young woman in her mid- to late- twenties in age, about five-feet, eight inches tall with brownish medium length hair. She has a medium brown skin complexion and light brown eyes. Her figure was like that of a model, a Halle Berry kind of body. She was wearing a medium-length dress, black in color, with skin tone stockings and black shoes. She walked into the apartment twisting her hips each time she stepped and went straight to the kitchen to view the table setting and the meal John had prepared. John followed her.

"Everything looks great," she said in a romantic voice.

"Thank you," John said. He pulled out a chair for her to sit on to enjoy the perfectly prepared meal. He then sat in a chair next to her. After eating the meal, John lifted his glass of white wine to her to make a toast.

"Here's to a long lasting relationship," he said. She raised her glass of wine up as well and smiled as both of their glasses touched. They both drank the wine in their glasses. She then got up out of her chair very slowly after setting her now empty glass on the table. He looked at her with sexual passion. She leaned down and gave him a passionate kiss. Afterwards, she pulled him from his chair and started to unbutton his shirt, then pants. He likewise did the same to her, all the while kissing each other. He opened her dress and exposed her breast. She did not have on a bra. They made their way to the bedroom, all the while kissing and pawing at each other. They then made passionate love to each other.

CHAPTER 4

Saturday morning rolled around. It was about eight o'clock in the morning. John woke up at the sound of his alarm clock. He then woke Kelly up.

"Good morning," he said with a smile and a kiss.

"Good morning. What time is it?" she asked him, now lying on her right side facing John with her head on a pillow. John looked over at his clock to get the time. He then turned back to her.

"It's eight o'clock," he said.

"Oh no!" she said as she pushed the cover off and got up out the bed. She was completely nude. "I have a luncheon with a couple of the city council members," she explained as she dressed.

"On Saturday?" John asked.

"Yes, some of us don't have the luxury of having their own business and setting their own days off," she said with a smile. She finally finished dressing, and then she hurried over to John as he lay in bed and kissed him lightly on the lips. He grabbed her and kissed her passionately. She kissed him back and realized again that she had to leave. "No, John, I really have to go," she said pulling away.

She sat on the bed and put on her shoes. "Will I see you tonight?" she asked.

"Sure you will," he said with a smile.

"Good, then I will call you later."

"Okay," he replied. Mayor Kelly then left the apartment. John shortly afterward got up, dressed and left his apartment to go to Spencer's place to pick him up for their plane ride. He arrived at Spencer's apartment at about ten a.m. He knocked on the door of Spencer's apartment. Spencer opened the door with coffee in one hand and a donut in the other.

"Come in, John," he said. "Have some coffee and donuts."

"No, thanks, but I would like to leave and get up into the wild blue yonder," John said pointing upward.

"Keep your shirt on, man. We have plenty of time for that." Spencer replied. Spencer took a few minutes to finish his coffee and donuts, grabbed his jacket and baseball cap, then went toward the front door of the apartment with John closely behind. They exited the apartment, jumped in John's car and off they went to the private aircraft airport.

CHAPTER 5

After forty-five minutes of riding, they finally arrived at the airport. A worker at the airport met them. His name was Frank Logan. Frank was an elderly gentleman in his mid-sixties with a gray beard, side burns and bald head. He is about five-feet, five-inches tall and is a heavyset man (weighing about 250 pounds). He has a dark complexion and smoked a cigar.

"Hi, Frank," John said with a smile, holding his right hand out to shake Frank's hand. Frank shook John's hand.

"Everything is ready for you, Mr. Savage," Frank replied.

"Good," said John.

"And he's flying with you, Mr. Savage?" Frank asked with a smile.

"Yes," replied John. "This is Spencer Lewis, my partner."

"Very nice to meet you, sir," Frank said, extending his right hand out to shake Spencer's hand. Spencer held out his right hand as well to shake Frank's hand.

"Call me Spencer," he replied. John, Spencer, and Frank approached the plane. It was a 2021, highly sophisticated twin engine plane. John went through the routine safety checks and inspection of the plane. After everything was to his satisfaction, they prepared to board the plane.

"Everything look good, Frank?" John said.

"Yes, sir," Frank replied. Then he left the two men and went to the control tower. John gave Spencer a parachute to wear in flight.

"A parachute?" Spencer replied nervously. "Are you expecting something to happen?"

"No, no, man, but it's better to be safe than sorry, and any way this is the procedure before taking a plane up." John said. "Everything looks okay. Let's climb in, bro, and get into the wide blue yonder," John said jokingly with a smile. They both climbed in the cockpit by a rope ladder.

"You sit in the navigator's seat, Spencer, and I'll sit in the pilot's seat." John proceeded to check all of the instruments in the cockpit. Spencer sat looking at John as he went about checking the instruments.

"Everything look okay, John?" asked Spencer.

"Sure," John said. "Just relax. You're in good hands. I have been flying for five years, so you have nothing to worry about."

Spencer had a look on his face as if he had something to tell John. He finally convinced himself that he needed to tell John of his fear of flying.

"John, I am afraid of flying," he said. "When I was a young boy, I saw my grandfather crash in an airplane and die. He was in the circus and was doing some flying stunts. Ever since then I said I would never fly in a plane."

"Don't worry, you are safe with me. We will not be doing any stunts and I will make sure we get back safe and sound." At that point John proceeded to put the headphones on his head over his ears. He directed Spencer to do the same with the other headphone set. Spencer placed the headphones over his ears just as John had instructed him to do.

"Blue bandit to tower, Blue bandit to tower, come in tower. Over," John said.

"This is tower. Go ahead. Over," the voice said.

"We are looking for clearance for takeoff. Over," John replied.

"You are clear to take off. Over," the voice said.

"Roger, out" John said, then he pushed the throttle forward slightly and the plane began to move forward. The plane finally moved in position to runway three. John checked with the tower once more to make sure everything was clear. He was given the go ahead; all's clear again. John looked at Spencer and said with excitement, "Hold on to your seat, buddy. We're going into the wide blue yonder!" John pushed the throttle all the way forward and grabbed the steering wheel with both hands. The plane began to move in a very fast motion. John pulled the steering wheel back to him and before long the plane had taken off into the sky.

CHAPTER 6

The two men had been flying now for thirty minutes.

"Man, this is the life up here in the sky away from everyone, the hustle and bustle of business, away from everything," John said.

Spencer finally settled down and started to enjoy the ride. It was a very clear day. There wasn't a cloud in the sky. The sun was out and bright. It was a wonderful day. John and Spencer had flown for another thirty minutes now and everything was fine. They had finally made it to the neutral zone, a patch of land that no one owned and that separated the two countries.

"Look at all that clear green. Too bad no one can inhabit it," John said.

"Yeah, it looks like good farm land," Spencer replied.

"Well, let's head back," John said. Spencer agreed. Suddenly the plane's engine started to sputter as the plane was making it turn.

"What's wrong?" Spencer asked.

"I don't know," John replied. John started to check the instruments panel as the plane began to lose altitude.

"Spencer, brace yourself!" John said with a nervous voice. "We are too low to jump." The plane hit a few treetops in its descent and went down in a somewhat clear area in the woods. Luckily the plane did not explode.

CHAPTER 7

After the dust and smoke had cleared, John and Spencer were unconscious. One hour had passed since the crash and John began to show some life. He regained consciousness and had a slight cut on his forehead. He pushed his body away from the steering wheel of the plane, and then grabbed his head gently. He moaned, and then looked around to find Spencer. Spencer was slumped over the instrument panel, still unconscious. John collected himself and then proceeded to revive Spencer. He pulled Spencer back into his seat away from the instrument panel and slapped him on the face gently a few times calling his name.

Spencer woke up, grabbed his head gently with both hands moaning, and asked, "What happened?"

"I don't know," John said. Then he began to inspect the plane's control panel.

"Where are we?" Spencer asked.

"In some wooded area," John replied, still looking at the instrument panel trying to determine what went wrong. Then he turned his attention to Spencer. "Are you hurt Spencer? Do you think you can walk?"

Spencer began to inspect his body parts. "I have a slight cut on the thigh part of my left leg, but nothing serious," he said.

"Well, let's see if we can get back to civilization," John said.

"That's fine with me," Spencer replied. They both proceeded to climb out of the wreckage. They both landed on the ground at the same time on their feet. Spencer went down on one knee. John went over to help him up to both feet.

"Which way should we go?" Spencer asked. John stuck his left hand pointing finger in his mouth, pulled it out and held it in the wind while still holding Spencer with his right hand. "This way," he said, pointing north.

"Lead on and I will follow," Spencer said.

"Are you sure you are all right?" John asked again with a concerned look.

"Yes, I am all right," Spencer replied once again. John released Spencer and started walking in the wooded part of the forest with Spencer closely behind. They wondered around the forest for a few hours.

"John, I have to rest. There seems to be no end to this forest," Spencer replied.

"Sure there is," John said. He then looked up at the sky and noted the sun has almost disappeared. "Let's camp here by this log and we will get a fresh start in the morning. Don't worry, Spencer. We'll make it out of here."

John looked around, grabbed some small sticks, and put them in a pile. He then grabbed two stones and struck them together to start a fire. Soon, both men were sitting next to the fire.

"John," Spencer said as he pulled the somewhat ragged jacket tightly around his body from the cool, damp forest air, "could I ask you a question?"

"Sure, man, ask away." John said. "How is it that you get all the women? I mean, I'm not a bad looking guy and it's hard for me to get a date. But you, well, you don't have to ask a woman for anything. They just give it to you. How do you do that? I mean, what do you say to get them in bed?"

"There's nothing I do or say. Well, you're just born with it, I guess," John replied.

"Well, you better be glad there is a cure for AIDS or you would be in big trouble."

"Amen to that," John said. "Hey, man, I'm going to get me some sleep now. I'll see you in the morning."

Good night," Spencer said.

"Good night," John replied, "and, man, I'm sorry I got you into this mess, talking you into taking this trip with me. But I'll make it up to you once we get out of here, buddy. I promise." Spencer didn't reply for he had lain down and gone fast to sleep. John lay down and went to sleep as well.

CHAPTER 8

Morning came as fast as the night. Spencer woke and found himself completely surrounded by a boa constrictor. The snake was a half a foot round in diameter and twenty feet long. John was still asleep. Spencer tried to free himself of the snake, but the more he struggled, the tighter the snake got around Spencer body. Spencer decided he needed help. He called out to John to help him, but the snake was getting tighter and tighter around Spencer's body. Spencer's face was turning black and blue and he was passing out when John woke up, turned to Spencer and saw what was happening. John quickly jumped to his feet and jumped in Spencer's direction, grabbing the snake by the neck with both hands. He then remembered the hunting knife he carried with him whenever he would go out on a flying trip. He frantically grabbed for the knife and pulled the knife from its holster. He stabbed the snake several times in the neck. The snake's blood was gushing out everywhere. Its blood was all over John and Spencer. After countless punctures into the snake with the knife, the snake fell dead. Spencer lay as though he was dead himself. John caught his breath for a moment, and then rushed to Spencer's aid.

John pushed the snake's body off Spencer, and then pulled Spencer away from the battle area. He sat on the ground and cradled Spencer in his arms. "Spencer! Spencer! Wake up!" John yelled, as he took a part of his unstained jacket and wiped the snake's blood from Spencer's face. From that action Spencer woke up, still believing that the snake was around him, and started to struggle.

"It's okay, man. It's okay. It's dead," John said as he tried to restrain Spencer. Spencer realized he was free of the snake and calmed himself. He looked at the snake to see what type of snake it was and how large it was.

"John, we have to get out of here today, man. I can't spend another night in these woods."

"Don't worry. We'll get out of here today," John said. John helped Spencer to his feet.

They continued their journey through the forest. Spencer spotted a berry patch. "Breakfast," he said and went toward the berries.

"Wait!" John yelled. "Let's look for snakes because berries draw snakes." Spencer stopped in his tracks and waited for John to investigate.

"All is clear," John said. Then they started to munch out on the berries. John and Spencer picked a handful of berries and sat on a nearby log. John looked around as he was eating the berries and noticed a tall tree near their position.

"I'm going to climb that tall tree over there to see if I can find a house or something," John said. "You stay here and rest a bit."

"Sure," Spencer replied, "I'm not going anywhere. Hell, I don't know where to go." John went over to the tall tree and started his upward climb. He finally reached the top of the tree and looked around. He spotted smoke at the northern part of the forest.

"I see smoke!" he yelled to Spencer. "Over that way," pointing to the north. John worked his way down the tree and went back to Spencer's position now still sitting on the log.

"Hey, man, where there is smoke, there are people," Spencer said.

"You got that right man. Let's go this way," John said pointing.

John helped Spencer up from the log to his feet and they started off in the direction where the smoke was spotted. They finally made their way to the edge of the forest. There they saw a farmhouse. Smoke was coming from the chimney.

"Civilization," Spencer said, with a bit of cheer in his voice. "Let's go and see if they have a phone that we can use so we can get the hell out of Dodge and get back home."

"I'm with you," John said. They started their walk toward the house. They had gotten within fifty yards of the house when suddenly a man came out of the house onto the porch. He was a white man, about middle aged, dressed in overalls and a wool brown jacket. John and Spencer saw the man and jumped to the ground.

"Aw, shit!" Spencer said in a low voice. "We are in the white nation!"

"Damn! How in the hell did we get here?" John said, in a low voice as well.

"Fuck that. How in the hell do we get out!" Spencer replied with excitement.

"I don't know, but we have to go back into that forest till nightfall, then we will try to find an empty house or apartment, something where we can get some food and clothing and a map. Then I believe we can find our way back home."

John and Spencer crawled their way back to the edge of the forest where they waited, hiding in the brush of the forest till nightfall.

CHAPTER 9

At about six p.m., they started out through the night in search of food, clothing and somewhere to lay their head. They passed by the farmhouse and came to a road. It was pitch dark and they could barely see each other.

"Which way do you think we should go?" Spencer asked.

"Let's head south. We saw what going north got us," John said.

"Right," Spencer replied.

CHAPTER 10

They walked for two hours and every once in a while a car would come by. John and Spencer would duck into the dark to avoid visual contact. They finally made their way to a somewhat populated community.

"What do we do now?" Spencer asked.

"Well, let's look for a house with all the lights out. Most likely no one will be home."

"Good thinking," Spencer replied. "Let's go."

They made their way into the community and came to a house with the lights on. The two men walked up to the house very slowly and cautiously and peeped in. They saw a white family sitting at the dinner table. The man looked to be in his mid-thirties and the woman in her early thirties. They have two children, a boy three-years-old and a girl nine-years-old. The drapes were pulled back. Because of that, John and Spencer could see everything in the house. The white man was sitting at the table facing the window. He was talking to his wife when he noticed a shadow move outside of the window. The white man slowly got up out of his chair, all the while talking to his wife.

"What's wrong?" she asked in a low voice. He motioned for her to keep talking. He left the room and returned with a double barreled shotgun. John and Spencer saw the man rushing toward the window and ran back into the dark as fast as they could. The white man then ran to the front door, opened it and ran out of the house to the front of his yard. He heard running noises and shot into the dark in the direction of the noises.

His wife came to the door shouting, "What's wrong! What's wrong! Larry?"

"I heard someone running over there," he said, pointing in the direction he was shooting with his shotgun.

"We might have some peeping toms at the window," she said.

"I don't think we'll have any more problems with them or him tonight," the man said.

"Come on back inside," the woman said. "We'll call the police and have them search the area."

Three other white men came out of their homes to Larry's yard.

"What happened, Larry?" one of them asked. They were all armed with shotguns as well.

"I think it was some peeping tom. I think I scared 'em off," Larry replied. "I'm going to call the police and have them patrol the area."

"Good idea," one of the other white neighbors said. "If there's someone out there, the police will catch 'em." They all went back into their respective homes. Luckily, neither John nor Spencer was hurt.

"Man, that was close," Spencer said.

"Yeah, too close," John replied. "Come on, let's see if we can find a house where no one's at home."

They started making their way through the neighborhood, being ever so careful not to be seen. Suddenly a police patrol car arrived on the scene shining its spotlights in various areas as it moved down the street. John and Spencer spotted the patrol car, ran to the closest house, and lay down on the ground next to the house in the shadows. The patrol car moved slowly past the house shining its spotlights as it passed.

"Stop here," one of the white policeman said, "I thought I saw something." He shone his spotlight in John and Spencer's location, but they were so flat against the ground that they were not seen.

"I guess it was nothing," the officer said. "Let's move on." The patrol car continued its forward motion down the street and moved out of sight.

"What do you think they will do to us if we are caught?" Spencer asked in a very low voice.

"They will kill us on sight," John whispered. Spencer now had a very worried look on his face. They both stood up against the house and noticed all the lights were out in the house. They moved to the back of the house and peeped through a semi-small window. There they found themselves looking into the kitchen of the house. Everything was quiet and calm inside. John looked around to find something to pry the window open, but could not find anything. They then went to the back door of the house. The door was made of wood with two peering windows. John pulled out his wallet and took out a credit card.

"Ha, the old credit card trick," Spencer said.

"That's right," John replied. He then stuck the card in between the door and the door jam. He pushed and twisted and pushed and twisted until he got the door open.

"Yes!" Spencer whispered with a sense of gladness.

"Now, we must be careful. Someone could be inside," John said.

"Right," Spencer replied. The two men entered the house, closing the door gently behind them.

"You stay next to the door, Spencer, and I will survey the area." John walked slowly and cautiously through the room. Spencer knelt down by the door, watching John's every move. John saw the refrigerator, went to it, and opened it.

"Food," he said in a low voice. There he found leftover chicken, ham, bread, dressing, and more. John pulled the drumsticks from the chicken, stuck one in his mouth, the other in hand, bread and everything else he could carry. Suddenly the kitchen lights came on. In the other entrance of the kitchen, a stocky, bearded white man with sandy hair past his shoulders was standing. He was in his mid-thirties and about six feet tall. John looked at the man as if he was looking at a ghost. Spencer was looking in horror as well. The white man was very surprised to see John and Spencer, two black men in his kitchen.

"What! What the hell…what are you two niggers doing here! How did y'all get here? How did y'all get in this country?" Neither John nor Spencer said a word. John dropped everything he had in his arms and hands and mouth to the floor. "I know y'all are here to spy. To find out how to take over our country. You are not supposed to be here in our country. Well, I'm going to stop you. You won't be going back to that nigger country of yours" the white man said.

He grabbed a large knife from the knife holder. "Now, nigger, I'm going to carve you up into nigger bits, then your partner."

The white man started his cautious approach toward John. John stood in a martial art-like stance. The white man jabbed at John with the knife. John jumped back. The white man tried again in the same fashion. John blocked his attempt, hit the man with a few fast punches, and then kicked him with a roundhouse Kung Fu kick. The knife went one way and the white man went the other way, both hitting the floor. At that same moment, another white man came to the same entrance of the kitchen. He was a slim man in his mid-thirties as well, with sandy hair to his shoulders and was clean shaven. He had a shotgun in his hands.

"What's going on here?" he asked. He saw John standing in his stance and Spencer at the back door. Then he looked at the floor and saw his brother lying flat on his face and food everywhere.

"You niggers, what are y'all doing here? What have you done to my brother?" he cried out angrily. He started to raise the shotgun to shoot John. John kicked the shotgun before he could aim and shoot it. The gun went to the floor.

"Run Spencer!" John shouted. Spencer opened the door and ran back out into the night with John close behind. The slim white man ran to the back door yelling, all the while shaking a fist in the air. "We're going to get you niggers! No matter where you run, we're going to get you!" The slim white man then went to his brother's aid.

CHAPTER 11

John and Spencer ran into a nearby ditch. Tired and scared, they both lay in the ditch, flat on their backs.

"Man, I know we have got to be dreaming. This is a nightmare," Spencer said panting for air.

"Then I'll be glad when we wake up," John replied. Ten minutes later a large number of different colored flashing lights appeared. John and Spencer looked over the edge of the ditch. There were four police cars parked in front of the house John and Spencer had run from.

"Man, we have got to find somewhere to hide," Spencer said. "If they find us, they are going to kill us."

"I know," John replied. John then cautiously looked around for another house that he hoped would be empty. He spotted a red brick house which was quite a distance away with all of its lights off. He then lay down in his original position.

"I think I have found another house I think is empty."

"Another empty house," Spencer said in a sarcastic way.

"Yeah, we either stay here and risk the chance of getting caught or we can make our way to that house which will give us more cover."

"Well, okay, John, let's try again," Spencer said. And with that, they both backed down to the bottom of the ditch and followed the ditch around near the red brick house. They finally reached a point in the ditch where they were parallel to the house. They then crawled up to the edge of the ditch, looked around to see if the coast was clear, then low crawled to the house. They made it to the back part of the house. This house was structured basically like the house they had broken into earlier. John got out his card again and, in the same way as before, proceeded to open the door. It worked. He and Spencer went in, cautiously closing the door behind them. And not a moment too soon for two white policemen came up to the house in which John and Spencer had taken refuge. John and Spencer lay flat on the floor against the wall as close as they could. One policeman shone a flashlight into the house through the window. He saw nothing. The other tried to open the door, but with John's quick thinking, he had locked the door after entering the house.

The police could not get in. The two policemen then moved on to the next house. John and Spencer breathed a sigh of relief.

"Man, I hope no one is here this time," Spencer said in a low voice.

"Me too. You stay where you are. I'll check to see if anyone is here," John said. He then got up carefully and moved throughout the house. Their luck had finally changed. No one was home. After his careful sweep of the house, he returned to share the good news with Spencer.

"No one is here," John said with a cheerful tone.

"Thank God," Spencer said with a breath of relief. They went to the refrigerator and ate everything edible.

"We've got to find a place to rest where no one will see us when they come in," Spencer said. John looked around. He then looked at Spencer. They both said at the same time, "The closet!"

"You take one. I'll take the other," John said.

"Sounds good to me," Spencer said.

"Even though we will be concealed, be cautious. Sleep with your ears open," John said. They both went into the closets.

CHAPTER 12

Eight hours later, about seven thirty in the morning, the owner of the house, a registered nurse, came home from a long night at work. She was about five feet, six inches tall and a brunette with shoulder-length hair. She has a Jessica Simpson-like body and face. She was in her early twenties. She stuck her key into the door's lock and opened it. Not noticing the kitchen, she went straight to her bedroom.

"Boy, what a long night," she said out loud. John heard her and woke up. He was in her bedroom closet. He put his hands over his face to wipe the sleep away. He then cracked the door open to see who was there. He looked at her as she was taking off her nurse's uniform and shoes. She still has on a white slip that covers her body. He knew she was coming toward the closet. He closed the closet door very gently, and stood up against the wall in the far corner of the closet. She walked toward the closet and opened the door. She stepped into the closet and knelt down to put her shoes on the floor. She stopped with her hand still on the shoes and looked slowly in John's direction. She realized he was an intruder and, worse than that, he was black.

She jumped up very quickly, threw her shoes at him, and ran out of the closet through the bedroom. John quickly ran after her and caught her before she could exit the bedroom. He wrapped one of his arms around her arms and body and placed his free hand over her mouth. She struggled to get free, but to no avail. Suddenly she stopped. John paused for a moment, still holding her.

"Look, we are not here to hurt you or anyone. If I let you go, do you promise not to try to run out or scream?" John asked. She paused for a moment then nodded her head in agreement.

"Okay, I am going to move my hands away, but remember you promised," John replied. He first removed his hand from her mouth, and then a few seconds later he removed his arm from around her body. She turned to look at him, not so much fear now but amazement, for she had never been this close to a black man before. She looked in his eyes and saw the fear deep within them.

"You said 'we,'" she replied. "Do you mean there are more of you here?"

"Yes, one other," he said. She went to the chair next to the bed and sat on the edge of it. John went to the bed and sat on the edge of it.

"How did you get here?" she asked. John paused, looked at the floor, and then looked at her again.

"My friend and I were flying my plane when we developed engine problems. Our plane went down in a wooded area not very far from here. We thought we were still in our country, but we soon found out we weren't."

"Does anyone else know you're in this country?" she asked. "Yes, we went to a house before we came to this one. There were two men there. They tried to kill us. We managed to escape. I think the two men called the police because they were searching for us last night. This is what forced us to come here. We are not spies nor are we here to take over your country; we are just two men who accidentally ended up in this country." He then leaned over and put his face in his hands. Susanna looked at John with compassion and sorrow.

"What's your name?" she asked in a calm voice. He took his hands from his face and looked at her again.

"My name is John Savage," he said.

"Pleased to meet you, John Savage. My name is Susanna Clark," she replied, putting out her hand for a handshake. John took her hand in his. He was amazed at the softness of her skin and that the whiteness would not rub off. She was also as equally amazed about the fact that his color would not rub off.

"Will you help us get back to our country? I don't think we can do it alone. We are not familiar with your country," John said in a pleading voice.

She looked at John for a moment, and then she nodded her head, signaling she would help. "Where is your friend?" she asked.

"He's in one of your closets," John said. "I'll get him." John got up from the bed and attempted to leave the room to find Spencer, when suddenly there was a knock on the front door. John stopped with a look of fear on his face. Susanna got up out of the chair and went to the bedroom entrance where John was now standing.

"Quick, get back into the closet," she said in a low voice. "I'll get rid of whoever it is."

John very quickly got back into the closet as he was instructed, hoping and praying she would keep her word and not turn them in. Susanna closed the closet door behind him. She went to the living room and put on a robe she had lying on the living room sofa. Then she cracked the front door open.

"Yes?" she said. It was one of the policemen who had been looking for John and Spencer last night.

"Sorry to bother you, ma'am, but we are looking for two niggers that have entered the country. Do you mind if I come in?" he asked.

Susanna hesitated, and then said, "Sure, come in, officer." She opened the door wide enough for him to enter. The officer looked around to see if there was some sign of John and Spencer being there.

"Please excuse my appearance but I just got off work," she said distracting the officer.

"I understand, ma'am. This won't take long. As I was saying, these niggers have entered the country and we think they are spies trying to take over our country. They are not supposed to be here. We can't let them destroy our way of life. Have you seen anything of them?" he asked.

She paused, taking in everything the policeman had said. John heard every word that was said for he had cracked the closet door open. John crossed his fingers in hopes that she would not go back on her word.

"No, I haven't seen them," Susanna replied. "but if I do, I will perform my duty and call the authority."

"Good. Then I will leave you. Sorry to have bothered you, ma'am. You have a nice day," the policeman said.

"No bother," she said as she walked him to the door. She opened the door to let the officer out.

"Well, bye now," he said smiling.

"Bye now," she said smiling as he walked out the door. She closed the door behind him. She then peered out of the front window to watch the officer get into his patrol car and leave. John was relieved to see she believed him and was a woman of her word. He came out of the closet and into the living room.

"Thank you for not turning us in and believing me," he said in a relieved voice.

"I am a pretty good judge of character, and I don't think you're lying. Your appearance indicates you have had some kind of accident," she said.

John looked at the clothing he was wearing. "Is it okay if I wash up in your restroom?" he asked.

"Sure," she said.

"Do you have any men's clothing here, something I can wear? I need to get out of these rags." he replied.

"I think I might be able to find something," she said. With that, John went to the bathroom that was connected to the bedroom. He closed the bathroom door behind him. He cut on the shower and began to take off the ragged, blood-stained clothes and underwear. He opened the shower curtain, stepped into the shower closing the shower curtain, and started to wash himself. A few minutes later the shower curtain quickly opened. Susanna was standing there completely nude.

John, startled a bit, looked at her standing still now as the water hit him all over his body. He was in a trance as was she. She finally stepped into the rear end of the shower and closed the curtain. She started rubbing John up and down his chest. John grabbed her with both hands, all so gently and slowly. He pulled her to him and kissed her lightly. They stared at each other for a moment with hot passion in their eyes. Then he gave her a long passionate kiss. He caressed her butt cheeks with both hands and she likewise caressed his. She then moved one of her hands to his penis. She was amazed at how large it was in diameter. She was afraid for a second, but the heat of the moment overcame her fear. She played with it for a while, stroking it back and forth until it had extended to its fullest length. John's penis was about ten inches long. She then backed up against the shower wall, pulling John with her. He leaned down and put the nipples of her breast in his mouth, all the while rubbing her vagina. She started to moan indicating her degree of pleasure with her back against the shower wall and arms now over her head against the shower wall. A few minutes later, Susanna turned facing the shower wall and bent over slightly. She then motions for John to stick his big black ten-inch penis into her now wet and soft white vagina. He did. With each thrust of his penis into her vagina, they both moaned. John's thrusting motions were slow and intense for the moment. Then without warning the thrusting motion became faster and faster, popping her buttocks with his body. In and out, in and out his penis went with him. He grabbed her waist and pulled her to him with each thrust. Suddenly Susanna started to scream with satisfied passion, and moments later John did as well. They had both reached an orgasm. They paused for a moment with fatigue while John's penis was still inside of her. He then pulled it out and she turned to face him. They then kissed passionately.

CHAPTER 13

They finished showering and they exited the shower.

"Did you find any clothes?" John asked. She went to the closet and found some clothing her ex-boyfriend had left. She pulled out a shirt and pair of pants. They just happened to be the right size for John. He put the clothes on, and then remembers his friend.

"Spencer," he said to himself in a low voice. "I forgot all about him." He went to the other bedroom closet where Spencer was located, still sound asleep. John opened the closet door and saw Spencer lying on the floor. He knelt down and shook Spencer to wake him up.

Spencer awoke, looked at John, and said, "Man, I had the worst dream I ever had in my entire life."

"That wasn't a dream, man," John replied.

"You mean, we are really here in the white nation?" Spencer asked. John nodded, signifying he was correct. Spencer's worries and fears returned. He stood up with the help of John and exited the closet. Susanna came into the room now fully dressed. Spencer saw her and jumped into a martial art stance.

"Look out, John!" Spencer yelled.

"Don't worry, man. She's on our side," John replied. "Susanna, this is my fearless friend Spencer Lewis."

"It's nice to meet you, Spencer," she said, extending her hand, all in the same breath. Spencer took her hand and shook it in acceptance of her friendship and help. He also was amazed at how soft her skin was and that the whiteness of her skin would not rub off. Spencer then turned his attention back to his friend.

"John, you look clean! I need to shower and change clothing as well," Spencer said.

"Sure," Susanna replied, "just follow me." She turned and walked to her bedroom. They both looked at her perfectly shaped well-built body. Then they looked at each other and smiled. Spencer proceeded to follow her.

CHAPTER 14

While Spencer was showering, Susanna was preparing breakfast for the three of them. She had pulled out another shirt and pants for Spencer to wear. John was sitting at the table.

As Spencer was showering, he could not help but wonder if Susanna was really going to help them or was she setting them up for the kill. Spencer finished shower and put on the clothes that were given to him. The clothing was a little bit too big for him. He then entered the kitchen where John and Susanna sat waiting for him. Spencer sat in an empty seat where a plate of food laid waiting. Spencer wasted no time eating the food. Neither did John. They even had seconds.

After the meal, Spencer looked at Susanna and asked, "Why are you helping us?"

Susanna looked at Spencer with compassion. "First, I don't think you and John are spies. You don't look the part. Secondly, there are a lot of whites that believe this continent should be as one like it once was. With everyone loving together and having equal rights."

"My great-grandfather heard this speech before and we didn't have equal rights," Spencer interrupted.

"That's true. I heard this from my parents as well, but I'm talking about real equal rights, where everyone is treated the same. I'm one of those whites who believe in this."

"Thank goodness," Spencer said. "Then how do we get out of here?"

"Y'all are about fifty miles from the border. We are in the heart of the city."

"The heart of the city!" Spencer said in a loud voice.

"Calm down man, calm down" John said.

"Yes," Susanna replied, "therefore we have to leave at night. I have a car we can use. With luck, we can make it to the border with no problems."

"Luck. That's one thing we don't have," Spencer said.

CHAPTER 15

With that, they left the kitchen and went to the living room. Susanna turned on the TV. A cowboy picture was playing. They sat down to watch the show. Then the show was interrupted by a newsflash. A well-dressed white woman appeared on the screen.

"Please excuse this news flash, but reports from our police department indicate there are two blacks in our nation. It is reported there are only two. Two men believed to be spies. If seen, please do not kill them. Capture them and turn them in to the police. A five-thousand dollar reward is given for the capture of these two men. We now return you back to our regular program."

The cowboy picture returned. John and Spencer looked at each other and then they looked at Susanna. She paused for a moment, thinking how nice it would be to have that five thousand dollars. Then she reassured the two men of her intentions.

"I am not going to turn y'all in. I gave you my word and I am not going back on it."

John and Spencer had a look of relief on their faces.

"Everyone in this city will be looking for us now," Spencer said.

"That's right, so we have to be extra careful," John said.
"I'm going to the clothing store to buy some black outfits for us to wear tonight," she said. "It would be very hard for anyone to spot us with them on at night."

"Good idea," John replied. She wrote John and Spencer's clothing sizes down on a piece of paper. She went to the bedroom, grabbed her purse out of the chair and went toward the front door. John met her at the door.

"Be careful," he said smiling.

"I will," she said, smiling back. She turned and opened the door to leave. She walked out the door closing it behind her. John watches her through the curtains as she walks to her 2054 Pontiac Ventura, gold in color, a good running car.

"You let her go like that. How do you know she's not going to bring those white cops back with her?" Spencer asked.

"Because she had a chance to turn us in but didn't. And anyway we have to trust her; she's all we've got." John replied.

"Are you falling for this woman? I see it in your face," Spencer asked. John looked at Spencer, not saying a word to that question. "If you have fallen in love with this woman, forget it. You can't stay here and you surely can't take her back to our nation. Our people will kill her too." John looked at the floor with a sad look on his face for he was deeply in love with Susanna.

CHAPTER 16

Two hours later, Susanna returned with bags in her hands. She set all the bags she had on the porch at the front door. She proceeded to unlock the door with her key. One of the neighbors came over to help her.

"Susanna!" the white man called as he approached her from across the street. "Need some help with those bags?"

"No, Bob," she said, "I can handle them myself." Bob was a young, long blonde haired, blue-eyed, Don Juan-kind kind of guy. He was about in his mid or late twenties in age and he was a weight lifter. He stood about six feet, five inches tall and was a very heavy man weighing about 270 pounds of pure muscles. He had been after Susanna ever since she moved into the neighborhood about a year ago.

"I'm not going to leave you until you let me help you," he said with a smile. John and Spencer heard what was said and went in Susanna's bedroom closing the bedroom door behind them. John stood against the door to hear what was going on. Spencer had hidden himself in the bedroom closet. Susanna turned to unlock the door, peeping in to see if the room was clear. She opened the door, grabbing a couple of bags, and went in. Bob followed with the rest of the bags. He closed the door after entering the house.

"Why will you not go out with me?" Bob asked putting the bags on the sofa.

"I've been very busy. Now if you will excuse me, I have to get ready for work." She grabbed him by the hand and led him to the front door. He glanced in the kitchen and saw a number of plates, glasses, and silverware on the table. He pulled away from her and went to the kitchen entrance.

"I didn't know you had guests last night. I didn't see anyone come or go," he said.

"Are you watching me!" she said angrily.

"Where is he?" Bob asked with a bit of anger in his voice. He went to Susanna's bedroom door. She tried to stop him, but could not. Bob opened the door and looked around the room. He found the ragged clothing that Spencer had taken off lying on the floor. Bob entered the bedroom. John was now hiding behind the open door. Bob picked up the rags, looked at them for

34

a moment, then looked in the mirror on the dresser. Bob saw a reflection of John behind the door. He turned quickly toward the door. John realized he had been discovered. Susanna was standing between Bob and the door.

"You bitch!" Bob said angrily as he looked at her. "You nigger-lovin bitch!" he continued with anger. Bob then struck Susanna across the face with the back of his left hand with a lot of force. So much force that it knocked her to the floor of the living room. John pushed the bedroom door over slightly, just enough to make his way from behind it. Susanna got up off the floor and moved back to the bedroom doorway.

"I'm going to collect the reward on you, nigger, but first I'm going to make you wish you had never come here," he said with as much hate as he could muster.

John stood in his martial arts stance once again, watching Bob's every move. Bob moved close to John, and then swung at him with all his might. John blocked the lick with his right arm and hit Bob square in the face with his left fist with the speed of Bruce Lee. Bob backed up, stood there for a second or two, shook his head, and then laughed.

"That's all you have, nigger?" he said. John took a step backwards. With a worried look on his face, he got back in his stance again. Bob stepped close to John again and swung at him. John blocked the lick again, and then hit Bob with a countless number of body punches. Bob stood there looking at John, laughing. Susanna was standing in the doorway with her hands over her mouth, hoping that John would win. Bob then hit John across the face with the back of his left hand, knocking John backward against the wall. He quickly grabbed John and locked his arms around John's body in a bear hug, squeezing John for every little breath of air he had in his lungs. He then released John. John, weak from the lack of air, fell to the floor. Bob then picked John up, held him over his head, and threw John across the room into the wall. John fell to the floor, out cold. Bob then turned his attention to Susanna.

"Now it's your turn, you nigger-lovin bitch!" He quickly moved to her location, grabbed her by the hair, and shoved her on the sofa. Spencer had gotten up enough nerve to come out of the closet. He looked over by the bed and saw his friend John on the floor unconscious. Spencer then walked to the bedroom entrance. Bob turned and saw him.

"Another nigger. How many of y'all are there?" he asked. "It doesn't matter. I'm going to kill you all."

Spencer slowly walked into the living room, starting to warm up using martial arts moves and gestures. Bob looked at Spencer and laughed. "You too, huh?" he said.

Bob moved closer to Spencer and swung at him. As in one motion, Spencer blocked the lick with his right arm, turned sideways and, with his left elbow, and hit Bob in the nose. Bob backed up and grabbed his nose with both hands. He removed his hands and blood was there.

Susanna was still on the sofa hoping that Spencer would win this fight. Spencer had positioned himself in his stance again. Bob was angrier than ever. He yelled as he rushed Spencer, trying to grab him in a bear hug just as he had done John. Spencer moved to the side and kneed him in the groin. Bob bent over grabbing himself. Then with both hands cupped together, Spencer hit Bob in the back of the neck as hard as he could. Bob fell to the floor on his knees and grabbed his neck. Spencer had position himself in his stance again. Bob then lowered his hands, turned, and looked at Spencer. Spencer, with a couple of martial arts round house kicks with his right foot, hit Bob in the face. Blood gushed from Bob's mouth as he fell back and hit the floor. Bob was out cold.

Spencer then went back into the bedroom to John's aid. He sat John up and leaned him against the wall. He slapped John lightly on the face a couple of times.

"Wake up, John. Wake up," Spencer said. John finally came to. John then grabbed his head with both hands.

"What happened?" he asked. Spencer helped John to his feet and took him into the living room. Susanna came over to help Spencer with John. They sat John on the sofa.

"Are you okay, John?" she asked. "I'm okay, thanks to super Spencer."

John saw the big white man lying on the floor unconscious. "You did that Spencer?" he asked. "I didn't know you were that good."

"All of that practice I put in paid off," Spencer said. "What are we going to do with big boy?"

"We are going to tie his big ass up," John replied.

"Wait, I have some rope out back," Susanna said and she went to get the rope, returning with it. They tied the big white man up and put a gag in his mouth. He was so heavy John and Spencer had to drag him to the closet. Susanna went to the bags of clothes where she pulled out the black pants, shirts, and hoods they were going to wear that night. John and Spencer returned to the living room.

"I don't know how we could ever repay you, Susanna, for what you are doing for us," John said. Then he pulled Susanna to him and kissed her lightly on the lips.

"That goes double for me," Spencer said as he also kissed Susanna.

"Well, we better get a little rest. There's a long night ahead of us," she said.

"You're right," John replied. John and Susanna lay in bed with the now black clothing on, arm in arm. Spencer lay on the couch of the living room.

CHAPTER 17

A few hours later, night came. Spencer woke first. He cleared his eyes. He then went to the bedroom where John and Susanna lay. Spencer woke them up.

"It's time to go," Spencer said.

"Right," John replied. John and Susanna got up and went into the living room where the other bags were.

"I bought backpacks with food, a compass and a pair of binoculars," she said.

"Very good, Susanna. You have thought of everything." John replied. They packed everything they were going to carry in the backpacks, and then went for the front door.

"Wait, let's check on that big dude," Spencer said. "I haven't heard anything out of him since the fight." They all went to the closet door. John opened it to find the big man lying there motionless. John knelt down to check his neck for a pulse. There was none. Spencer, without knowing, had broken the guy's neck.

"He's dead," John said.

"What?!" Spencer replied.
"His neck is broken," John said. John stood up. They walked out of the closet and closed the closet door. John looked at Spencer who had a sad look on his face.

"It was either him or us. Come on, we have got to get out of here and back to our own country," John said, putting an arm around Spencer. Susanna went to the front door, opened it and then went out on the porch. She looked around to see if anyone was outside. There was no one in sight. She then went back into the house.

"Wait until I get into the car and open the back door. Then y'all come out and get in." "Right," John said. Spencer nod, indicating approval. Susanna went to the car, got in on the driver's side and opened the back door as she had said. John and Spencer went out on the porch, closing the front door behind them and rushed to the open door of the car with backpacks in hand. They entered the car and closed the door.

"Now get down on the floor so no one will see you and cover yourselves with this large blanket." She gave John a large blanket she already had in the car and they covered themselves.

She started the car and backed out of the driveway. She then moved down her street. She took the skullcap off her head and placed it on the seat next to her. Susanna had driven thirty blocks when the car began to sputter. She looked at the car's instruments panel and noticed the gas hand sitting on empty. "Dammit!" she said.

"What's wrong?" John whispered.

"I think we're out of gas. I forgot to put gas in this damn car earlier today." The car engine stopped and she let the car coast on its own to a complete stop next to the curb. Susanna then looked around to see if she could spot a gas station nearby. She turned off her headlights. Up the road five hundred yards from their position was a gas station.

"I see a gas station," she said in a low voice. "I'm going to go get some gas so we can continue on. Y'all stay down and quiet." Just as she began to open the driver's car door, a police car drove up directly behind her car. Two policemen got out of the patrol car and approached Susanna's car. One policeman went to the driver's side, while the other went to the passenger side of the car.

"Is everything okay, ma'am?" the officer on her side asked. Suddenly the officer noticed a slight bit of movement in the back part of the car.

"What is this?" he said grabbing his flashlight, shining it into the back part of the car. Both officers at the same time went to open the back doors of the car. The car doors flew open, knocking both officers down to the ground. John and Spencer jumped out. The policeman on John's side went for his gun, pulled it out of his holster and shot at John. John ducked, grabbing his backpack at the same time, and threw it at the gun-held hand. The force and heaviness of the backpack knocked the gun out of the policeman's hand and the officer fell to the ground. John then grabbed the officer by his shirt with both hands and pulled him from the ground. John then backhanded the officer with one hand, hit the officer with a few punches in the stomach, then hit the officer in the face again with a left cross. The officer hit the ground again.

Spencer was doing battle with the other policeman as well. Susanna sat frozen in her seat watching everything. John and Spencer both were victorious and ran off in the dark between two large buildings. The officer that John fought regained his faculties, jumped up from the ground, and went to the patrol car to call for help. The other officer went to the driver side and pulled Susanna out of the car, handcuffed, her and put her in the back of the patrol car. Within a matter of minutes, three more patrol cars arrived. There were two policemen in each car. All of the policemen in the cars jumped out with guns in hand.

"The niggers went in that direction, between those two buildings," yelled one of the first two policemen. The policemen broke up into twos under the direction of the police sergeant who had just arrived. The sergeant, a tall man, about six feet, eight inches tall is a very huge man as well, weighting about 310 pounds, mostly muscle. He was in his late forties in age and had black hair. The policemen went in the direction indicated to look for John and Spencer in the alley. Susanna sat in the back of the patrol car looking as they walked toward the alley. One of the first two policemen and another policeman that had just arrived stayed with Susanna.

As the policemen searched the alley, the one policeman who was first on the scene said, "Watch out. Those niggers can fight pretty good. They know that martial arts shit." The group continued to search the alley. John and Spencer were hiding behind a large barrel in the alley against the wall of one of the buildings. At the back of the alley was an eight-foot wall. John looked in the back of the alley and saw the brick wall. Spencer did too.

"We need to make a break for that wall," John said.

"Let's go," Spencer replied. They jumped up and ran for the wall. One of the policemen saw them and shone his light in their direction.

"There they are!" he yelled. "Stop!" Another yelled, "Or we will shoot." John and Spencer stopped as they were told and stood facing the wall with their hands in the air.

"Now turn around slowly," the other policeman said with their flash lights shining at them exposing their whole bodies. They turned around as they were told with hands still in the air. The sergeant and the other three policemen finally arrived with their flashlights shining at John and Spencer as well.

"So, y'all are the two niggers everyone is looking for," the sergeant said. "They don't look so tough."

"Well, let's see how tough they really are," one of the officers said.

"Yeah, let's see," the sergeant replied, pointing at one of the officers. "You, stay back and watch. Make sure they don't get out of this alley alive if they win."

"Sure," the officer said with a smile on his face and a hand on his gun.

"The rest of you take off your gun belts and take out your billy clubs." They did as they were told.

"Let them win," John whispered to Spencer.

"Now let's see how good you are," the sergeant repeated. John and Spencer lowered their hands and stood in their natural battle stance. The policemen closed in on them. They fought, but the police overpowered them, hitting John and Spencer with their billy clubs. After the fight, John and Spencer were handcuffed and dragged to the patrol cars where the other two policemen and Susanna was waiting. John was thrown into the back of one car and Spencer was thrown into the back of another patrol car. The sergeant got into his car and called in to the police station.

"Home base, this is Adam nine. Over," he said.

"This is home base. Over," a female voice said from the radio speaker.

"We have the two niggers in custody and we are on our way back to the station. Please inform the chief. Over."

"Will do. Roger out," the voice said.

The sergeant started his car and signaled for everyone to follow him.

CHAPTER 18

After arriving to the station, Susanna, John and Spencer were pulled out of the cars and led up the short flight of stairs into the building. As they entered the building, everyone stopped what they were doing to look at the catch of the century. They all crowded in the semi-large entrance hall of the building.

"All right, all right, what's going on?" a man said as he made his way through the crowd of policemen.

"Here they are, chief," the sergeant said. The police chief looked at John and Spencer. "Man, I haven't been this close to a nigger since the Great Race War," he said with a smile. Police Chief Jeff Morgan was in his early seventies and had gray hair on his head and a gray mustache. He was about five feet, nine inches tall, had a medium body size weighing about 170 pounds. He was a no nonsense kind of guy and believed in following orders. Then he looked at Susanna.

"Who is this girl?" he asked.

"She was with them," the sergeant said.

"I was kidnapped…" Susanna yelled out.

"You'll have your chance to tell your story later," the chief interrupted. The chief looked around and told everyone to break it up and return to work. Then he told the sergeant and the two officers to escort the prisoners to their jail cell. The sergeant grabbed John by the handcuffs and led him off to the jail. The other two policemen did the same to Susanna and Spencer. The sergeant opened a jail cell door and pushed John inside so hard that he fell to the floor. They then led Spencer to the next jail cell and likewise pushed him in. Susanna was placed in a jail cell as well. The sergeant looked at John and Spencer, smiled at them as if though to say "you're dead meat." Then he told the other two policemen to leave. They did and he followed.

John got up off the floor and sat on the bunk against the cell wall. He then wiped the blood out of his nose with his shirtsleeve, although his hands were still cuffed. Spencer did likewise. Spencer then came over to the bars that separated the two cells.

"What are we going to do?" Spencer asked.

"I don't know. Let's just sit back and see what happens," John replied. As John and Spencer lay back on their bunks, the police officers of the station walked by their holding tank, looking at them every five minutes with amazement. They also looked at Susanna, who was three cells down from John and Spencer.

CHAPTER 19

At about nine a.m. the next morning, John woke up because of the sound of voices coming from his cell window. John got up and went to the barred window. He saw a few white men, women and children standing in the car-length wide alley, hoping to get a look at the two unusual prisoners sitting in their town's jail.

"Look! There's one of them in the window," one woman yelled. They looked, murmuring words to each other and taking pictures. Then Spencer woke up.

"What's going on out there?" he asked.

"There's a crowd of people out there," John said.

Spencer got up and went to his window.

"There's the other nigger," a woman yelled. The crowd looked at Spencer and took pictures of him as well. Then the police chief, the captain in charge of the police station, and the mayor of the city came in the jail and stood in front of John and Spencer's jail holding tanks looking at them. John and Spencer looked back at them. Neither John nor Spencer said a word. The mayor is a short man about five feet, six inches tall and is slightly heavy for his height, about 170 pounds with slight potbelly. He was in his mid-fifties and had salt and pepper hair. The captain was about five feet, eleven inches tall and had an average build, weighing about 205 pounds. He had reddish hair.

"Where is the girl?" the mayor asked.

"Down this way, sir," the police captain replied pointing in the direction of the jail cell she was kept. They went to Susanna's cell and looked at her. She looked at them.

"I'm innocent," she said, "Innocent." Then she looked down at the floor.

"Take her down to interrogation room one," the captain said. The jailer opened Susanna's cell door and led her to the interrogation room. The police chief, captain, and mayor followed. After arriving to the room, the jailer removed the handcuffs from Susanna's wrist, and then left the room closing the door behind him.

"Sit down, Miss...." the mayor paused.

"Clark, Susanna Clark," she replied.

"Ms. Clark," the mayor continued. "Please." He pointed at the chair he wanted her to sit in. He pulled the chair out from under the table and motioned for her to sit. Susanna sat in the chair as she was instructed.

"How did you meet these two men?" the mayor asked.

Susanna paused, looking down at her hands as she was clutching them. "Yesterday morning, I came home to find these niggers in my home. One of them grabbed me and tied me up. I could do nothing, I was helpless," she said sobbing.

"How many more are there?" the chief asked.

"These two are the only two I have seen," she replied.

"Why are you dressed in those clothes?" the mayor asked.

"They made me wear these clothes and took me as a hostage. They even killed one of my neighbors who was trying to save me," she said. Then she started to cry. The mayor and police chief looked at each other, and then looked at Susanna again. The mayor handed her a handkerchief. Susanna wiped her eyes with the handkerchief.

"Did they say why they were here?" the mayor asked.

"They just kept saying they had to get back home, to their country." Susanna replied.

"Huh," the police chief said. Then he asked, "Did they have anything with them, some kind of weapon they were taking back with them?"

"No," she replied.

"Where is the body of your neighbor?" the chief asked.

"He's at my house in my bedroom closet tied up," she said.

"Why tie him up?" asked the captain.

"Because they wanted to make sure he didn't get out and alert anyone."

The mayor, chief and captain paused for a moment with the questioning. Then the mayor said, "Thank you very much for your cooperation Ms. Clark."

"Am I free to go?" she asked.

"Well, the chief here will go by your house to confirm your story. If your story checks out, you will be released," the mayor replied. The captain went to the door and signaled to the jailer to come and take her back to the jail cell. Susanna got up out of the chair and went back to her jail cell with the policeman. They did not put the handcuff back on her. She stopped and looked at John and Spencer as they lay on their bunks. Then the policeman gently directed her to move on.

"I want you and a couple of other officers to go to her house and check her story. Search the house completely for anything that can shed some light as to why those niggers are here," the mayor said.

"I'll get right on it, Mayor," the chief said. The chief took the arresting sergeant and another officer with him.

CHAPTER 20

Thirty minutes later, they arrived at Susanna's house. The sergeant opened the door with Susanna's house key, the key they had taken away from her during her arrest. The sergeant and the trooper entered first with guns drawn, then the chief followed. They looked around the living room.

"Sergeant, you take the kitchen. Troop, you take the back bedroom, and I'll take the master bedroom. Search everywhere and leave nothing unturned," the chief said. The two officers both nodded. "Let's go," the chief said. They all went to their respective rooms, turning over bed mattresses, and pulling out and searching drawers. Then the police chief went to the bedroom closet and opened it. There he found, just as Susanna had described, Bob's body all tied up, face down. The chief placed his left hand on Bob's neck to see if he could feel a pulse. But there was none. The chief then pulled his hand away, looked at the body, and then paused as if he was trying to figure out what happened. The chief went back to the living room where he met the other two officers.

"Did y'all find anything?" the chief asked.

"No, sir, not a thing," the sergeant replied.

"Me either, sir," the other officer said.

"There's a stiff in the master bedroom closet, just like the woman said."

The sergeant and the other officer went to the bedroom closet to see. The chief went to the phone and called the morgue to pick up the body. He then called the police station. The phone rang.

"Precinct 67," the voice said.

"Let me speak to the captain," the chief demanded.

"This is he," the voice said.

"This is Chief Morgan. Is the mayor there?"

"He's right here, sir. I will put you on the speaker. Go ahead, chief," the captain replied.

"Sir, we have just searched the house and found the body just as she said. I think she is innocent because her story checks out," the chief said. "

"Did you find anything else?" the mayor asked.

"No, sir, nothing out of the ordinary," the chief replied.

"Well, come back to the station. We'll have a little talk with those two niggers and get the information we're searching for."

"Yes, sir, we're on our way." The chief went to the master bedroom door, "Let's go back to the station gentlemen."

"Yes, sir," the sergeant said. They all left the house, locking the door behind them. They got into the patrol car and went back to the station.

CHAPTER 21

Twenty minutes had passed and they arrived back at the police station. Reporters and cameramen were standing in front of the police station.

"If they ask you anything, tell them 'no comment,'" the chief said.

"Yes, sir," they both replied. They got out of the car and were mobbed by the reporters and cameras.

"Who are those niggers in there?" one reporter asked.

"Again, no comment," the chief replied as he and the other two officers made their way through the crowd of reporters and TV cameras, up the steps and into the station. The chief pointed to two troopers.

"You and you, make sure those reporters don't get through that door."

"Yes, sir," they replied and went to the doors to secure them. The chief then told the sergeant to accompany him to the captain's office. They entered the office where the captain and the mayor were waiting. The mayor looked at the chief and said, "Let's have a talk with our two friends." He had an expression of anger on his face.

The chief turned to the sergeant. "Go and get the lighter one and take him to interrogation room three," the chief said.

"Yes, sir," the sergeant said with a slightly sly smile on his face. The sergeant left the room and went to the desk of the trooper who had gone to Susanna's house with him. "We have to take one of the niggers to interrogation room three. If he makes a false move, I want you to beat him with your club."

"Yes, sir," the trooper said. The trooper got up out his chair and they went to John's jail cell. John and Spencer were lying on their bunks, each in his own jail cell.

"Open the door," the sergeant said. The trooper opened the door and then pulled out his billy club and held it in both hands. Spencer sat up on his bunk to see what was going on. John sat upright on his bunk as well.

"You stay here, trooper. I'll bring him out," the sergeant said. He entered John's cell.

"All right, nigger, let's go."

John paused, and then stood on his feet. The sergeant grabbed John by the handcuffs and pulled him out of the cell. The pressure of metal to flesh was hurting John's wrists. John's displeasure of the sergeant pulling him was expressed on John's face. The sergeant led John to the interrogation room. The sergeant opened the door and pulled John into the room. He then pushed John into a chair. The trooper entered the room and stood guard.

"Now, you stay in that chair and don't you move, boy," the sergeant said. John did as he was told, looking at the sergeant with a frown on his face and hate in his eyes. The police chief and the mayor were still in the captain's office along with the captain.

"I want you to release the girl, captain, and then accompany us to question the nigger," the mayor said.

"Yes, sir," the captain said.

"Let's go, chief," the mayor said. With that, the mayor and chief went to the interrogation room.

The captain went to the jailer and instructed him to release Susanna and to get her a ride home. The captain then went to the interrogation room.

CHAPTER 22

The jailer went to Susanna, opened the jail cell door and told her she was free to go. Susanna got up off the bunk and exited the jail. She walked past Spencer, looking at him as he sat on his bunk behind the bars. Spencer looked at her with sadness and anger on his face as she passed by his cell. Susanna went to the personals desk to pick up her belongings. She then left the station with a trooper to go home. They went out of a back door of the station to avoid the reporters, which were still out front.

CHAPTER 23

John was sitting very still in the chair watching the sergeant's every move and the trooper at the door, all the while resting his arms on the table. The mayor and chief entered the room. The trooper guarding the door let them pass. The sergeant stepped back against a wall in the room to let them pass and position themselves on the opposite side of the table from John. The mayor and chief looked at John with amazement, wondering how he and Spencer came to be in their country and why. Moments later the captain entered the room.

"What's your name, boy?" the mayor asked in a crude voice. John looked at him, still with that angry look on his face. But he said nothing.

"I said, what's your name, boy?" the mayor repeated in a louder voice slapping both hands on the table. John, still looking at the mayor, said nothing.

"You might as well cooperate with us. Make it easy on yourself," the chief said, in a gentler voice than the mayor. John then focused his attention on the chief, finding somewhat of an ally among the three white men.

"My name is John Savage," he replied.

"John! That's a good wholesome name," the chief said.
"Where are you from in your country, John?" the chief asked.

"I'm from Los Angeles," he replied.

"Los Angeles. I remember Los Angeles back in the day, a fun filled city, full of movie stars and bright lights and..."

"Why are you here?" the mayor asked angrily, interrupting the chief, now at this time sitting in a chair next to the table.

John looked at the mayor, now frowning again. "We are here by accident. We flew over the neutral zone and ended up in your country. Our plane crashed in a wooded area, somewhere around here. I don't know where, but I know it's a wooded area. All we want to do is go back home."

"Why were you flying over the neutral zone?" the mayor asked.

"We wanted to see what the neutral zone looked like. That's all," John said.

"Why did you kill that man at the lady's house you broke into?" the chief asked.

"I didn't kill him…"

"Your partner did, huh, boy?" the mayor said interrupting John.

"The man attacked me for no reason at all," John continued. "I fought him but I was no match for him. He picked me up and threw me across the room against the wall, leaving me unconscious. When I came to, the man was lying on the floor. Tied him up so he wouldn't tell anyone we were there."

"And what about the girl?" the captain asked.

"We made her help us." John then looked up at the police chief. "We didn't mean to kill anyone. We only want to return to our country peacefully." Then John put his face in his hands as he shed a tear.

"All right, sergeant, take him back to his cell. Then bring the other Nigger," the mayor continued. The sergeant grabbed John by his handcuffs, pulling him out of the chair, and leading him back to his cell with the trooper who was guarding the door accompanying him.

"So, do you believe what he was saying, chief?" the mayor asked.

"He was very convincing," the chief said. "He could be telling the truth."

"What about you, captain?"

"I wouldn't trust them as far as I can throw them. I think they're up to something," the captain replied. The sergeant entered the room with Spencer in the same manner he did with John. They motioned to Spencer to sit in the same chair that John had sat in moments ago.

"What's your name, boy?" the mayor asked.

"My name is Spencer," he replied.

"Spencer. That's it?" the mayor asked. Spencer didn't say a word, looking down at the table with his cuffed hands in his lap.

"Why are you here?" the chief asked. Spencer still didn't say a word.

"What are you after in our country?" the captain asked.

"How did you get here?" the mayor asked. But Spencer still said nothing. The mayor signaled to the sergeant to hit Spencer with his billy club. The sergeant walked over next to Spencer and hit him in the back as hard as he could. Spencer felt the pain rush throughout his body; he flinched a bit but did not move out of his chair. The sergeant hit Spencer again in the back several times with all his might. With pain shooting throughout his body after each blow, Spencer merely sat there with tears in his eyes, thinking to himself that today he was going to die. The sergeant with a mighty blow hit Spencer in his hung down head. Blood spurted out of his head at the spot he was hit. His head fell to the table with blood spilling on it. He was slightly unconscious. The sergeant started to hit Spencer again, but the chief stopped him. Then the chief instructed the sergeant to take him back to his cell. The sergeant motioned to the trooper to assist him. They helped Spencer back to his cell, dragging him all the way. The other policemen were looking to see what had happened as they passed. The chief followed.

When Spender was being returned to the jail cell, John saw what had happened to him. "Would you put him in here with me, sir, so I may tend to his wounds?" John asked the chief.

The chief motioned to the sergeant to put Spencer in the same cell as John. "Thank you sir," John replied. The trooper opened the cell door and they dragged Spencer into the cell and laid him on the floor. They took the handcuffs off Spencer and John. John started to examine the cut in Spencer's head while he was still lying on the floor of the cell. He took one of the pillowcases and tore it up to make bandages. John wrapped the strips of cloth around Spencer's head to stop the bleeding. He then picked Spencer up from the floor and laid him on the bottom bunk. The bleeding had stopped and Spencer lay there motionless.

CHAPTER 24

The chief went back to the interrogation room. "I think we should check out the story of the one called John," the chief said. "He could be telling the truth."

"Whether he's telling the truth or not, you know and I know we can't let them return to their country," the mayor replied looking at the two men.

CHAPTER 25

Susanna finally arrived home.

"Do you need any help with anything?" the trooper asked.

"No, I'll be all right, thanks," she replied. Susanna got out of the police car and went into the house. The trooper drove back to the police station. There she saw everything turned over and pulled out. The house was a shambles. She went into her bedroom and opened the closet and found bloodstains where Bob's body once laid. She then lay back on her bed to bring into focus what has happened to her in the last two days of her life and to realize that she had fallen deeply in love with John. She started to cry.

CHAPTER 26

After her tearful cry, she got up off the bed and went through the house picking up clothing and straightening up what the police had done. After she finished, she called her friend's house. Nancy is Susanna's closest and dearest friend. Susanna could tell Nancy anything. Nancy is a young, longhaired, blonde, in her mid-twenties and very intelligent. She is an average looking woman weighting about 150 pounds with a height of about five feet, three inches tall and she wore eyeglasses. The phone rang.

"Hello" Nancy said.

"Hi, Nancy, this is Susanna."

"Susanna, are you all right?" Nancy asked in a concerned voice.

"Yes, I am all right but I need you to do me a favor."

"What kind of favor? You sound like something is wrong. What's wrong?" Nancy asked

"I need you to come to my house and I will tell you everything, but I need you to come now. Can you come now, Nancy?"

"Sure I can, sweetheart. I am walking out the door right now. I will see you in a few minutes," Nancy replied.
"Thank you, Nancy. You're the best," Susanna said.

They both hung up the phone.

CHAPTER 27

Fifteen minutes later, Nancy arrived at Susanna's house, got out of her car and went to the front door. Susanna opened the door to let her in. Nancy hugged Susanna.

"Susanna, are you all right?" she asked.

"Yes, I am," Susanna replied.

"I saw your picture on the news and my heart almost stopped. How do they look? Did you touch them?"

"Nancy, I need you to help me get my car back."

"Okay, where is it?" Nancy replied.

"It's parked about three miles from here. I ran out of gas." Susanna replied.

"Okay, let's go and get it." Nancy said. They both walked out of the house closing the door behind. Then they went to Nancy's car, got in, and took off.

"Nancy, I have a secret, and I don't want you to tell anyone. I mean not anyone, not even your family."

"I won't tell anyone Susanna, honest!"

"Well, one of the black men whose name is John, I have fallen in love with him."

"What! How?" Nancy asked.

"Yesterday morning when I got off from work, I found the one name John in my bedroom closet. I tried to get away, but he caught me. He told me what had happened and how they came to be in our country." Susanna paused for a moment then she continued. "Later on that morning, John and I took a shower together and we had sex, I…"

"What! Are you crazy?" Nancy said interrupting her with an excited and disappointing tone in her voice. "You can't have a life with a black man in this country, nor can he have a life with you in his country. And what if you are pregnant, what are you going to do then?"

"Well, I will have to deal with that if it happens," Susanna said.

"The best thing for you to do is put him out of your mind," Nancy replied.

"I know, I know and I've tried, but I can't." Susanna said with tears in her eyes. They finally arrived at the gas station to get the gas for Susanna's car.

"You stay here. I will get the gas for the car." Nancy said. Susanna smiled slightly, indicating her agreement to Nancy's statement. Nancy got out of the car, went to the trunk, and pulled out a gas can. She then went in the station to buy the gas. Susanna was still crying because of the love and hurt she felt for John. Nancy purchased the gas, put the gas in the trunk of her car, and continued on to where Susanna's car had stopped. She was looking at Susanna with a look of helplessness on her face, for she could not console her friend. They finally arrived at Susanna's car. Nancy got out the gas and put it in the tank of Susanna's car. Susanna helped. After they finished, Susanna hugged Nancy.

"Thank you for helping me out. I don't know what I would have done without you."

"Are you going to be all right?" Nancy asked. "I think I should stay with you until you get through this."

"No, I'll be all right. I just need time to think by myself," Susanna replied. Nancy paused, looking at Susanna. She put both of her hands on Susanna's face, and then smiled.

"Well, call me if you need me friend," Nancy said. Nancy then hugged Susanna once more and looked at her as if to say you really need me, but instead turned and walked away. She then got into her car and drove away.

CHAPTER 28

Susanna looked into her handbag, got her keys, got into her car and drove away as well. She went back to the gas station to fill her car's tank. She pumped the gas into her car's tank then went inside to pay the clerk.

"That will be fifteen dollars," the clerk said. She gave him the money. He looked at her and noticed she was the white woman that was kidnapped by the two black men. "Hey! You're the lady that was taken by the niggers! How do they look up close? Were you afraid?" Susanna turned and ran out of the store as fast as she could to her car and left the gas station. She drove straight home. She ran inside, closed the door, and rested against it for a moment. She then went to the sofa, laid her purse on it, and went to the kitchen. She fixed herself a drink, which consisted of vodka and orange juice, then went back to the living room and sat on the sofa. She turned on the TV. A movie had just gone off and the news was coming on.

"And here is the news. At the top of our news today, the two black men that were caught and jailed are scheduled to die tomorrow in the electric chair." Susanna saw their pictures flashed on the screen. "The police still do not know why or how they got here. The police do know the two black men won't be leaving here alive. The public is invited to witness the execution. This will be the first time since the Great Race War that a black man has died in our city's electric chair. In the other news tonight, the governor..."

Susanna turned the TV off and thought about what was said on the news. "Executed! I've got to get them out some kind of way," she said out loud. She sat there with her drink in hand, trying to determine how she was going to help them escape for the task looked almost impossible. She laid her drink on the coffee table and went to her bedroom. She searched for her dark glasses and wigs she sometimes wears. She put a wig on her head and noticed she looked different. She then put on the dark glasses. She hardly recognized herself. She went to the living room, grabbed her purse from the sofa and went to the store to replace the supplies the police had taken away earlier. No one recognized her. After buying all she needed, she went straight to the police station where John and Spencer were being held. The media and a small crowd of people were still standing out front of the police station.

Susanna drove up and parked her car two hundred feet away from everyone and sat there in her car, looking at the police station, trying to find a way out for John and Spencer. She decided to get out of the car and look at the station more closely. No one there recognized her. Susanna looked at the station again and noticed there was no way she could get them out. She then noticed an alley that ran next to the station. She decided to go into the alley. As she walked down the alley midway, she noticed windows with bars on them. Ahead of her, she noticed a few people standing there. She approached the small crowd.

"Why are y'all standing here?" she asked a man standing there with camera.

"I'm here to get a picture of the niggers they have in jail."

"Niggers," she said with a voice of surprise.

"You haven't been listening to the news!" he said. "They have two niggers in jail. Spies I believe, and they're in those two cells." He pointed as he talked. Susanna looked at the windows he was pointing at and she noticed a shadow moving in the second window. She turned and went back to her car and drove off. She went to a hardware store to get a long strong chain, and then she went home. After Susanna arrived home, she went to her bedroom and took off the wig and dark glasses. She looked in the mirror at herself, trying to get up the courage to do what she needed to do to save John and Spencer from death. She then took off her clothes, put her nightgown on, and lay in bed.

CHAPTER 29

One hour later, Spencer regained consciousness. "Oh, my head," he moaned, grabbing it. John was standing at the bars of their cell looking around and went to Spencer.

"Are you all right?" John asked, now sitting on the bunk next to him.

Spencer paused. "Yes, I guess," he finally replied.

"What happened to you? Why did they beat you like that?" John asked.

"I don't know. They were asking questions I didn't have answers to. So I didn't say anything and they started beating me," Spencer replied.

"Damn their souls," John said. "These peckerwoods are just like our grandparents said they were, dirty sons of bitches." John continued with anger, "I told them what happened and why we are here in their country, but they're not listening!"

Spencer merely looked at John with his hands on his head.

CHAPTER 30

The jailer came in with food for the prisoners. "Here is your food, niggers," he said as he pushed the food through the slot of the jail door.

"My name is not nigger!" John replied as he grabbed the tray of food. "It's John."

"Well, it's going to be dead after tomorrow." The jailer replied. John and Spencer looked at the jailer with worry on their face. "That's right. Y'all are going to die tomorrow," he said in a nasty tone. He laughed, and then walked away. John and Spencer looked at each other. John gave Spencer a portion of the food and they slowly started to eat.

CHAPTER 31

Hours had passed and the alarm clock went off. It was ten p.m. Susanna woke up and turned the alarm clock off. She went to the restroom and dashed water on her face to gain her composure. She grabbed a face cloth and wiped her face. She went to the living room where she had put the bags of clothing and items she had bought for the trip ahead. She pulled a set of the freshly bought clothing out of one shopping bag and put them on. She then packed the new backpacks she bought with food, water, and other items they might need. She went to her car with backpacks in one hand and the chain in the other and put the backpacks on the backseat of her car and the chain on the floor in the front of the car on the passenger side. After loading the car with everything she needed, she put on her wig again, looked at herself fully clothed in the mirror. She took a deep breath, and left the house. She went to the car, started it up, and left to save John and Spencer from certain death.

CHAPTER 32

Minutes later, Susanna arrived at the police station where John and Spencer were being held. She stopped the car on the other side of the street from the police station, almost in the same spot she was in earlier in the day. She sat for a moment looking at the station and noticed that everything was calm and quiet. All of the reporters, cameramen, and spectators had left for now. Susanna started to make her attempt to free John and Spencer, but at that moment, two police officers came out of the station. She froze. The officers, talking to each other, went down the sidewalk to their patrol car, then left. Susanna, now very nervous, looked around again to make sure the coast was clear. No one was in sight. She took a deep breath, started up the car, and went into action. She turned the car around calmly, and then backed up into the alley. Once she got in the alley close to the window where John and Spencer were being held, she turned the car off. She had turned off the car lights. She got out of the car with the chain in her hands. She looped the chain around a rod under the car and attached the end of the chain to itself. The chain had a hook on each end. She then grabbed the other end of the chain and went to the barred window, where John and Spencer were kept.

"John, John," she called out in a very low voice. John and Spencer heard the call. John went to the window and looked out of it.

"It's Susanna," he said to Spencer in a low voice as well. "Susanna, what are you doing here?" he asked in a low voice. At that moment Spencer had joined him.

"I am here to get y'all out," she said.

"How are you going to do that?" John asked. Spencer continued to look on.

"I am going to wrap the end of this chain around the bars and pull them out with my car," she replied.

"Good idea," John said with happiness. "Let me go to the cell door to see if anyone is coming."

"I'll go," Spencer said. Spencer moved to the cell door and looked around. No one was there. "The coast is clear," Spencer whispered. Then John repeated what Spencer had said to Susanna.

"Good," she replied. She then wrapped the chain around the bars of the window with John's help. She then hooked the end of the chain to itself, the same way she did under the car. "Now, as soon as I pull these bars out, y'all haul ass out of there and jump in the car so we can get out of here without getting caught." John agreed with her. She went to the entrance of the alley to make sure no one was out there. There wasn't a person in sight. She returned to her car, got in, and started the car. The sergeant decided he would work a double shift and was sitting at his desk reading. Another trooper and the jailer were there as well at their desks reading. Susanna quickly put the car in drive and hit the gas pedal. The car took off and pulled almost the entire cell wall down. Everyone in the station heard the noise.

"What tha' hell?" the sergeant asked. He and the other two men jumped out of their chairs very quickly and went to see what had happened. John and Spencer ran out of the cell as fast as they could and jumped into the car. Spencer jumped in the back seat of the car and John in the front seat, next to Susanna. John was halfway in when he told Susanna to go. She started moving and John jumped the rest of the way in the car. Susanna pulled out of the alley with lighting speed and made a quick left turn dragging half of the jail wall behind them. The force of the turn closed the car door for John.

The police officers found a big hole in the cell wall and found John and Spencer gone. They ran to the front of the station out into the street and saw the back lights of Susanna's car.

"You, trooper! Go and put out an APB on those two niggers and a white bitch. Tell them to set up roadblocks on every street, every road that leads out of town. Have them check every car that approaches their road block. Go!" yelled the sergeant.

"Yes sir," replied the trooper and he went as quickly as he could to do as he was instructed. They all went back inside the station and the sergeant rushed to his desk, picked up the phone, and called the chief. The phone rang, and rang, and rang. Finally the chief answered.

"Hello," he said in a half sleepy voice.

"Chief, the niggers have escaped!"

"What!" said the chief, fully awake now. "How did they escape?" he asked.

"Someone pulled the cell wall out where they were in and they escaped. I think it was that damn bitch that was with them," said the sergeant. "I've already put out an APB on them and we should be hearing something soon."

"Good work, sergeant, I'll be over as soon as possible," the chief said.

"Very good sir," the sergeant replied. And with that, they both hung up. The chief immediately called the captain and the mayor. He explained the situation to them and advised that they meet him at the police station as quickly as possible.

CHAPTER 33

The police roadblocks were quickly put into place.

Susanna, John, and Spencer had made it out of the city limits and were going out of town on a dark and deserted road. "Susanna, stop the car for a moment so I can disconnect the chain from the car." She stopped the car. John quickly jumped out of the car and disconnected the chain and jumped back in again. She started moving again. "Susanna, I want to thank you for saving our lives," John said. And with that, he kissed her on the cheek.

"I want to thank you, too," Spencer said with excitement, for he was very glad to be out of that jail. Spencer put his arms around Susanna's neck, hugging her in appreciation for all that she had done to help them.

"Well, fellows, we're not out of the woods yet. I'm sure they have road blocks up all around the town on every road by now," she said. And just as she had finished speaking, sure enough there was a roadblock straight ahead of them. One patrol car was blocking the road. Two policemen were there with the car. Susanna stopped the car. They were about fifty yards from the roadblock. "We've got to get by them," she said. "This road leads to the border of our two countries." They all three paused and looked at the police car with the red and white lights on top of the car flashing.

"You move over here where I am, Susanna, and I'll drive. I'll get us by these cops," John said. John got out of the car and went to the driver's side. Susanna moved over to the passenger's side. John got in the driver's seat. "Susanna, I want you to get down on the floor. You too, Spencer, and I'm going to drive us by those assholes," John said. "Get down now!" And with that said, Spencer and Susanna did just what John has said. John gripped the steering wheel tightly, and paused for a moment. Little beads of sweat has formed on his face. He then took a deep breath and hit the gas pedal.

The car took off like a bullet, charging toward the patrol car. The two policemen standing in front of the patrol car noticed Susanna's car racing at them at full speed. The two officers started firing their guns at the car. Bullets were ripping the car apart. John hunched down real low to keep from getting hurt.

The two policemen saw that the car was not stopping and ran for cover in a nearby ditch. Susanna's car hit the front of the patrol car. The force from the impact sent the patrol car spinning off the road. Sparks went everywhere.

But Susanna's car continued on. The two policemen quickly ran out of the ditch and continued shooting at the car in the night. One officer went to the patrol car, opened the door, and radioed in what had happened and gave their location.

CHAPTER 34

John sat up and looked back to see if the police were following. He saw nothing.

"Is everyone all right?" John asked.

"I'm okay," Susanna said, still crouched down on the car's floor.

"I'm all right, too," Spencer replied, also still down on the floor of the back part of the car.

"Y'all can get up now. They are not following us." John said. Susanna got up off the floor and sat in the seat. Spencer did likewise. Both of them looked back to see if they were being followed.

CHAPTER 35

They traveled twelve miles down the road when the engine went dead.

"What's wrong with the car now?" Susanna asked.

"I don't know," John replied. The car coasted to a stop along the side of the road.

"Do you have a flashlight Susanna?" John asked.

"Yes, in my glove compartment," she replied. She opened the glove compartment and pulled out the flashlight, turned it on, and gave it to John. They all got out of the car to see what was wrong. When they were all standing in front of the car, John shone the light on the grill of the car. The policemen had shot three holes into the radiator and all of the water had leaked out.

"Well, the car is done for," John said, still shining the light on the radiator.

"How far do you think we are form the border?" Spencer asked.

"It's hard for me to see. It's too dark. But I would say another five, ten miles." Susanna replied.

"Then let's take everything of value and what we can carry and hike our way to the border," John said.

"Good, let's go," Susanna replied. And with that everyone grabbed a backpack.

"This one is mine," she said, taking the backpack from Spencer, "I have my lady things in here."

"Okay," Spencer said. She gave Spencer the backpack she had grabbed at first. They grabbed everything they could carry and started off into the woods.

The dispatch took the call, wrote the information down, and gave it to the sergeant. The sergeant read it.

"Damn those black, dirty ass niggers," he said in an angry voice. The Chief was now entering the police station and went to the captain's office. The captain and the mayor shortly arrived after the chief and went to the captain's office as well. One of the troopers went to the sergeant and told him the Chief, the captain and the mayor has arrived. He then took the message to the captain's office to give it to the chief.

"Sir, I have a message from one of the road blocks. The niggers and that woman are heading for the border, down highway 159 East," the sergeant said. The chief took the paper and read it with concern on his face, then gave it to the mayor.

"What happened?" the captain asked.

"They got past a road block," the chief said looking at the captain.

"Well, I think we need to call out the National Guard to help us in this matter," the mayor said. At that point the mayor left the room.

"Sergeant, you and three other men go out to where they were spotted and see if you can pick up their trail. And when you do, radio back in your location," the captain said.

"Yes sir," he said with a smile on his face. The sergeant left the room. "You three come with me," he said pointing at the three officers that were standing by. They walked out of the station, got into two squad cars and took off to the fugitives' last known location.

Meanwhile, John, Spencer and Susanna had moved off a distance into the woods. They traveled about a quarter of the mile toward the border and stopped to make camp. They were traveling parallel to the road their car had broken down on.

"We'll make camp here," John said.

"Okay," Spencer said. "I'll get some wood to make a fire."

"No! No fires. That can be seen for miles. It will be light very soon anyway," Susanna said, looking up at the sky. There was nothing but stars and a full moon. The night was clear and the air was cool and only the sounds of the wild could be heard.

"We can all sleep here, next to this fallen tree," John said. The other two agreed. They laid their backpacks down next to the fallen tree. Then, they lay down on the ground using the backpacks as pillows and looked up again at the stars. Susanna was lying between John and Spencer.

"You know, sometimes I wonder why this continent was divided like it is now," Susanna said, as she looked at the stars. "You two are the first black men I have ever seen or touched in my entire life."

"And you are the first white woman we have ever seen up close and touched as well," John replied. "But it wasn't always like this. My grandfather told me long time ago this continent or nation was one. Everyone lived together under one president, under one rule. There were mixed marriages. Blacks marrying whites, and whites marrying blacks, Mexicans marrying whites, and so on. He told me racism took control of the whites and they started beating and killing blacks for no reason at all. This continued for ten years. The blacks decided they would take no more and armed themselves. The nation, the streets became a battleground. Every race shooting at each other. He said a lot of men, women, and children died on both sides during the Big Race War. The leaders of each race decided we needed to split the country up. Each race needed to have its own country. To live with their own people, they said. This is what we have today," John said with a sad tone.

Spencer sat up and looked over at John with sadness in his heart as well. Susanna also sat up and looked at John with a sad look on her face.

"What do your people think of whites?" Susanna asked.

"Our people hate whites because of what they did to us in the past," Spencer replied. "Our people will do just as your people; they will kill any white on sight that appears in our country."

Susanna looked at Spencer with sadness and disappointment on her face.

"A lot of people lost families members in the Big Race War and people just can't forget that," Spencer continued. There was a slight pause.

"Well, we need to get some sleep. We have a long day ahead of us," John said. And with that, everyone laid back and went to sleep.

Some minutes later, the sergeant and the troopers with him arrived at the position of the two officers that shot at the fugitives. They all got out of their cars. The two officers walked over to the sergeant and his men.

"What direction did they go?" the sergeant asked. One of the officers pointed in the dark, down the road. "Okay, you two take them back to the station. My driver and I will go ahead and try to pick up their trail. Let's go," he said. Everyone got into their cars. The sergeant and his driver went on down the road in the same direction as the fugitives. The other four policemen went back to the police station leaving the wrecked patrol car on the side of the road. About twenty minutes later, they arrived at Susanna's shot up, broken down car. They pulled up behind it with their headlights still on. They shone their spotlights into the wooded area, which surrounded them, but saw nothing. Both of them got out of the car with guns drawn and flashlights in hand and gave the car a good once over. They noticed all of the bullet holes in the car's body, windshield and radiator. They were both standing in front of the car.

"They couldn't have gotten very far, because it's mighty dark out there," the trooper said.

"Maybe you're right," the sergeant said. They both went back to the patrol car. The trooper opened the door of the car on the driver's side and sat down, then closed the door. The sergeant went to the passenger side and did likewise. The sergeant radioed in their finding.

"This is Adam 92. Come in home base. Over."

"This is home base. Over," the voice said.

"Let me speak to the chief," he said.

"Wait one moment. Out," the voice said. There was a pause. "This is the chief, Adam 92. Go ahead. Over."

"Chief, we're out here on highway 159 East. The car has been disabled, but there is no sign of anyone. Over."

"Where do you think they went? Over." the chief asked.

"I think they went into the woods and they are trying to make their way to the border. I don't think they are moving now because it is so hard to see out here, even with the moonlight. The trooper and I are going to stay out here in the patrol car the rest of the night. We only have a few hours left before daylight anyway and then we will start our search for them at first light. Over."

"Good idea, sergeant. The National Guard will be at your location first thing in the morning to help with the search. Over."

"Yes, sir, we'll be looking for them. Over and out." The sergeant hung up the radio hand mike. "Well, trooper, all we have to do now is lay back and get some sleep. We'll start our search at first light."

"Yes, sir, I'll get in the backseat and get some sleep," the trooper said.

"Go ahead," the sergeant replied. The trooper got in the backseat of the car, pulled his billy club out, and laid it on the floor of the car. He then laid his body across the seat.

"I'll get those niggers back," the sergeant said in a very low voice. He then lay down in the front seat of the patrol car. In no time, the both of them were sound asleep.

A few hours later, daylight finally broke through. It was about seven thirty in the morning. Susanna was the first to wake up. She sat up and wiped the sleep from her eyes. She then looked around at her surroundings. She saw nothing but tall trees, weeds, grass, and bugs flying through the air. She then looked at John and Spencer, one on each side of her.

"Wake up, fellows," she said, shaking them both.

"What! What!" they both said and jumped up ready to fight. Susanna was frightened at their reaction to her waking them up. They both realized it was only Susanna wakening them and not the enemy. They both relaxed.

"We're sorry, Susanna," John said, "but we are so tense that everything sets us off."

"And I think we will continue to be like this until we get home," Spencer said. "I will go and get some firewood so we can make breakfast."

"That's a good idea. I am a little hungry," John said. Spencer left to look for sticks of firewood. Susanna got up on her feet and went to John. She put her hands on his face and looked him in the eyes.

"You are going to make it. I have no doubts that you will make it back home," she said with strong convictions in her voice.

"But what about you? How are you going to make it here now? I know the police are aware that you are the one helping us. I feel very bad leaving you here to face them all alone," John said.

"Don't worry. I have friends that will help me make it here," she said with a smile on her face. She then kissed him with passion. He kissed her back. Moments later Spencer returned with small sticks of wood in his arms. He saw what was going on. A slight look of jealously rolled over his face as he stood there watching from a short distance. The expression converted back to its normal self. "Here is the firewood, you two," he said. They stopped kissing, then went to their backpacks and pulled out the food that was there. Susanna pulled out some matches she had in her backpack and gave them to Spencer to start the fire.

The daylight woke the sergeant up as well. The sergeant sat up, got out of the patrol car, stretched, and then looked around for clues as to where the fugitives went. He noticed some broken twigs on a small tree a short distance from the road. He went to the tree to examine it. He then looked around and found signs of foot prints. He then went back to the car and got the trooper.

"Trooper, wake up, wake up." The trooper got up wiping the sleep from his eyes.

"What's wrong?" the officer said.

"I have found the direction they went. Let's go see if we can find them." The officer sat up and looked at the sergeant through the car window.

"Where?" the trooper asked.

"Over there," the sergeant pointed.

"Don't you think we should wait until backup gets here?" he asked.

"No!" the sergeant said angrily. "We are going to get those niggers ourselves. Now get out of there and let's go!" The sergeant opened the car door. The trooper got his billy club and away they went in the direction of John and the others.

John, Spencer, and Susanna were sitting around the fire eating their breakfast. The two policemen were quickly closing in on their position. Suddenly Spencer heard an unusual noise.

"Wait!" Spencer said holding up one hand, "I heard a noise."

"What kind of noise?" John asked.

"Someone stepped on a stick."

The sergeant and the trooper smelled food. They drew their guns. "You go in that direction, and I'll keep straight ahead. We will catch them by surprise," the sergeant said. The trooper moved off in the direction he was told. The sergeant moved up slowly and cautiously, looking as he walked, with gun pointed. The sergeant noticed a little smoke ahead of him. Suddenly he saw the fire and the backpacks, but no one was around. He walked toward the fire, passing a tree. Suddenly John jumped out from around the tree and kicked the gun out of the sergeant's hand. The gun hit the ground. Then John got in his battle stance and was about to attack the sergeant.

"John!" Spencer yelled, "Let me. I owe him something." John stepped back. Spencer took the bandage from his head and threw it to the ground. He started going through his martial arts gestures. The sergeant pulled out his billy club, and then smiled. "I'm going to kill you this time, nigger." The sergeant ran at Spencer with his billy club, swinging it back and forth to hit him. Spencer ducked and dodged every time the sergeant swung the club at him. Spencer spun around and kicked the sergeant in the chest. The sergeant stumbled backward a bit and grabbed his chest. The sergeant came at Spencer, again swinging the club. Spencer blocked the club with his arm, wrapped his arm around the club, all in one motion, and then hit the sergeant in the chest again with a karate blow as hard as he could. The sergeant grabbed his chest with both hands this time and went to his knees. Spencer then hit the sergeant in the face with a roundhouse kick. Blood shot out of the sergeant's mouth as he fell to the ground. Then suddenly the trooper approached the scene pointing his gun.

"Look out!" Susanna yelled. Hearing the yell made the trooper nervous. The trooper, in his nervousness, fired his gun as it was aimed in John and Spencer's direction. John fell backward and hit the ground. Susanna moved out from around the tree with a gun in hand, raised it and fired it at the trooper hitting him. The force of the bullet knocked the trooper backward. He fell to the ground motionless. The sergeant went for his gun, which was lying near him. He grabbed the gun and turned to shoot Spencer. Spencer ran as fast as he could, jumped in the air and gave the sergeant a flying kick; the sergeant fell backward to the ground, dropping the gun again. Blood shot out of the sergeant's mouth once more. Spencer then grabbed the sergeant by his head with both hands and, in a swift motion, broke his neck. Susanna went to

77

John's aid. She knelt down on her knees and pulled John off the ground into her arms.

"John, John!" she cried. But John did not respond. Spencer then went to their location, stood over them looking with tears in his eyes. Susanna hugged John crying. John then opened his eyes. Everything was blurry for a moment, and then his vision cleared.

"Susanna, I'm all right," he said in a very low voice. Susanna stopped hugging him, and then looked at him.

"You're alive!" she cried. Spencer knelt down and hugged the both of them. The bullet had grazed John's head.

"John, are you sure you're all right?" Spencer asked.

"Yes, I am," John replied.

"Then we had better get out of here before someone else comes," Spencer said. He ran over to where the backpacks were and grabbed them all. He then stamped the fire out. Susanna helped John to his feet.

"John, I had to kill that sergeant guy. He was going to..."

"Don't worry about it," John said interrupting Spencer. "I'm sure he gave you no choice." John looked over at the sergeant's body, and then he looked at the trooper's body.

"Let's go," Susanna said. And with that, they left.

An hour later, the chief and the National Guard arrived. They saw Susanna's car and the patrol car parked behind it. The guardsmen jumped out of the truck. The leader, a captain, and the chief arrived in a jeep. There were about 20 guardsmen armed with M16s and in full military gear. The National Guard captain and the chief looked around. The chief and the captain noticed broken twigs and pressed down weeds leading to the woods. They went to the beginning of the reasonably made trail to examine it further.

"Looks like they all went in this way, sir," the captain said.

"Yes, it does seem so," the chief replied. "Let's go in and see what we can find." The captain ordered the guardsmen to form a single file behind him. They did and followed the trail, first the captain, then the chief, then the rest of the national guardsmen. A few minutes later they came upon the disbanded camp. They found the sergeant's body. The chief and the captain examined his body, while the others looked around. In their examination, they found the sergeant's neck was broken.

"This is a job of a real killer," the captain said.

"Sir, over here!" a guardsman yelled. The captain and the chief went over to where the guardsman was. He had found the trooper. "He's still alive," the guardsman said. The chief knelt down to checked the wounded trooper. The trooper moaned with pain. The chief found a bullet hole in the trooper's shoulder.

"Do you know which direction they went?" the chief asked the trooper.

"They went that way," the trooper said, pointing in pain.

"Okay, trooper, just relax," the chief said. The chief stood up with the captain. Two guardsmen tended to the trooper. "Captain, could you have a man help me take my man to the patrol car? There I can radio in for an ambulance to come pick him up and my sergeant body."

"Yes, sir. The rest of us will go after those murdering bastards," the captain continued. The captain ordered a man to help the chief with the trooper. The captain then ordered the other guardsmen to huddle around him.

"Men, we are going after those bastards. They are traveling east toward the border. They have about an hour on us so we are going to have to move at a fast pace to catch them. I want a search line formed, and then we will travel east as well. Are there any questions?" the captain asked. No one said a word. "All right, men. Let's move out." With that the guardsmen took their positions and moved eastward at port arms.

"Sir, here is a filed radio report," the captain said, giving it to the chief. "I will keep you posted on what is happening."

The chief grabbed the radio. The captain rejoined his men. The National Guardsmen were moving at a fast pace, searching and checking every bush, looking up every tree. Several hours had passed. John, Spencer, and Susanna had made their way to the border. John and Spencer had joy in their faces and eyes as they looked over at their country. John and Spencer hugged each other and then they hugged Susanna at the same time.

"I'm so glad to see our country," Spencer said with joy. "I thought at one point we would never see it again." They continued to look over at their homeland. They noticed a wide river dividing the two countries and military men along the border on both sides. They also noticed two guards at the entrance of the bridge on the white side.

"We are going to have to make our break now," Spencer said looking at John.

"I know," John replied in a sad voice now realizing he was going to have to leave Susanna behind.

"I'm almost sure there are people following us," Spencer continued. John looked at Susanna. He walked up to her and put both his hands on her face.

"I would love to take you with me, but my people would never accept you in our country. They would kill you and I couldn't live with that," John said. Tears were rolling down Susanna's face. "Maybe one day in the near future, our nation will come together again as one. That day I will come looking for you, my love, to spend the rest of my life with you." At that point, tears started rolling down John's face. He moved his face to hers slowly and kissed her on the lips lightly, then pulled back looking her in the face once again. She reached into her belt and pulled out the gun she had used earlier.

"Here John, you are going to need this to get past those guards." She gave it to him. John accepted it and put it in his belt. Spencer came over to Susanna and hugged her, slightly teary himself. He kissed her on the forehead and pulled back with both hands on her shoulders, looked at her, then smiled. He then walked off from Susanna, saying "Let's go, John." Spencer now walked toward the bridge through the tall weed and bushes.

"You stay here among the trees and bushes where no one will see you," John said. "Are you going to be all right?"

"Yes, I have some friends that will help me." John looked at her for one last time. Then he walked off at a fast pace to catch up with Spencer, all the while looking back at Susanna. She waved goodbye at him. He waved back. They were some distance from her now and very close to the road that led to the bridge.

"There they are!" someone yelled. Gunfire rang out. John and Spencer started to run with bullets flying all around them, hitting trees, the ground, and all around. The guardsmen were shooting at them. They had finally caught up. John and Spencer ran as fast as they could with bullets flying everywhere. They finally reached the road. The guardsmen were in hot pursuit. John and Spencer were approaching the bridge. The two border guards saw them approaching and pulled their M16's off of their shoulders. They were preparing to shoot John and Spencer when John pulled the gun out of his belt that Susanna had given him and shot the two guards. They fell to the pavement. John and Spencer ran passed the fallen guards onto the bridge. Another border guardian manned the bridge's entrance.

"Run, Spencer, run," John yelled, both men now running at full speed. A third border guard got in a prone position. The guardsmen were still running toward the bridge. The border guard aimed his weapon, and then paused for a moment. John and Spencer got midways the bridge. The guard fired, hitting Spencer in the back, Spencer fell to the pavement and rolled a few feet. John looked back and saw that Spencer had been shot. He stopped and ran back to help his friend. The guardsmen, still aiming, fired again, hitting John in the chest, just as he had gotten to Spencer's position. John fell to the pavement still grabbing for his friend, who was lying face down on the bridge, with blood protruding from his back and eyes closed. The border guard and half of the National Guardsmen and the captain were running onto the bridge toward John and Spencer, unaware of what was going on at the other edge of the bridge. They reached John and Spencer.

John, lying on his back, looked up at the white military men. The sun was beaming in John's face. He could barely see the men. They all aimed their weapons at John and Spencer preparing to shoot when suddenly a large number of clicking sounds were heard. They sounded like a chain of rifles loading. The group of white men turned their attention from John and Spencer and focused their attention on a large number of black men in military clothing. There were about fifteen of them with their weapons aimed directly at the white men. Behind this group of fifteen black soldiers was a black major standing in a tank, looking at the white men with a serious stone face. The white captain saw what they were up against and ordered his men to back off, going back to their side of the bridge. The major signaled to four black soldiers with stretchers to get John and Spencer and carry them back to the black nation.

www.ingramcontent.com/pod-product-compliance
Lightning Source LLC
Chambersburg PA
CBHW052034260626
47163CB00006B/299